DANIEL
DISCOVERS
DANIEL

by

John M. Barrett

Illustrated by Joe Servello

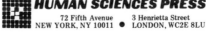
HUMAN SCIENCES PRESS

72 Fifth Avenue   3 Henrietta Street
NEW YORK, NY 10011 ● LONDON, WC2E 8LU

For
Al
Marion
Knowl
and
Darrell

Copyright © 1980 by
John M. Barrett
Printed in the United States of America
9876543210 987654321

Library of Congress Cataloging in Publication Data

Barrett, John M
Daniel discovers Daniel

   SUMMARY: Sure that he isn't loved because he
receives so little attention from his father, Daniel
determines to make a bond between them.
   [1.   Fathers and sons--Fiction.   2.   Identity--
Fiction]   I.   Servello, Joe.   II.   Title.
PZ7.B27518Dan   [Fic]   LC 79-17897
               ISBN 0-87705-423-7

Daniel was quiet most of the time. He loved to read and to sort and arrange the unusual stamps in his collection. Many people, including his parents, thought he was shy. But Daniel wasn't shy. He simply didn't feel like talking.

Although Daniel didn't say much, he knew a lot—from his books and from his stamps, but most importantly from watching people. Daniel could tell how his mother was feeling before she said a word. When she smiled and her eyes sparkled, he knew she would do almost anything for him. He never asked for much, only for money to buy stamps or for her to let him make brownies or go to the library.

Daniel tried to be fair and not greedy. He was different from his younger brother, Peter. Peter always wanted more, and he got everything anyway, especially from their father. Peter was picked up and thrown into the air. He went for rides on their father's shoulders. After work, their father was excited to see Peter. His eyes showed it. So did his voice.

Their father always said to Daniel, "Oh, hi Daniel. How was school today? Are you reading any good books?" He always said it, but he never seemed to care what Daniel answered. Even worse, he never hugged Daniel the way he hugged Peter. Not even when Daniel kissed him goodnight.

One day after school Daniel was having some ice cream with his mother. As he was finishing up the last bit, suddenly he said, "Mom, why does Dad love Peter more than me?"

His mother's mouth opened. She looked at Daniel's shirt instead of his face, and then she said, "Your father loves you both the same. It's just that Peter's only seven—he's still a little boy, like a teddy bear. You're nine. You're not so little anymore. When you were younger, Dad treated you the same way he treats Peter now."

Daniel knew this wasn't true. He remembered waiting for his father to pick him up and squeeze him when he was a little boy. It never happened, or he'd remember. His father was always too busy, too tired, too something —until Peter was born. Daniel had begun to wonder if he had a real father somewhere else.

Daniel was imagining finding his real father when his mother said, "Peter loves sports and ball games. So does your father. If you'd watch the games on television or play ball in the backyard, you could be with Dad like Peter is."

Daniel gave his mother a little hug. "Thanks Mom," he said. "I'm going out to ride my bike."

"Be back for dinner," she replied, kissing him on the cheek. "Have fun." She looked a little worried.

Daniel got on his bike and rode, not knowing where he was going. When he wanted to get out of the house he did that. He liked the feeling of being surrounded by moving air, of getting tired going up hills, and then coasting, coasting all the way down. But today he didn't notice.

Today he knew why his father loved Peter and not him. His father and Peter were alike. His mother had said so. It was so simple he wondered why he hadn't thought of it himself. It was so simple, but how could he change?

He hated watching sports on television. It was so boring that he always had to read a magazine or book at the same time. He had tried to care about the leagues, teams, players, standings, scores, playoffs, and everything else, but it just didn't matter to him. He couldn't remember any of it.

Playing sports was even worse. He could never admit it to anyone, but he was afraid of the ball. He was afraid it would hit him in the face, or that he would miss it, or that once he had it, he wouldn't be able to throw it all the way back.

His mind and body did not work very well together. Peter and his father did everything so easily. He had to stop, think, and tell his body what to do. Even then, his body didn't always do what he said. The only time his body worked well was when he was on his bike. His bike was his friend.

Daniel looked to the left and noticed he was passing his teacher's house.

It looked like no one was home.

"I wonder where Mr. Johnson is," Daniel thought to himself. "Probably still at school, making more tests to torture us. Boy, I'm glad I have him. He's so fair and funny. We're the only class doing a whole play ourselves. I can't wait."

Daniel checked his watch. It was time to head for home. When he got there he learned that his brother had been invited to Billy's house for the night. "Oh great!" Daniel thought. "Now Dad will pay some attention to me."

After dinner Daniel said, "Dad, would you help me sort through my stamps tonight? I have some new ones to put in my album."

His father's voice came from behind the newspaper. "I'd like to, Daniel, but I'm tired, and I have a report to finish. Maybe some other time."

"When?" Daniel asked.

"We'll see," his father answered.

Daniel saw his mother give his father a quick, angry look. "Can I help you, Daniel?" she offered, smiling at him.

"No thanks, Mom," he answered. "I'm kind of tired too, from my bike ride. Maybe I'll just read."

"Would you like to ask someone to sleep overnight?" she asked.

"No thanks," he said, shaking his head.

Daniel went upstairs and laid down on his bed. He tried to read, but he couldn't keep his mind on the book. "Dad will never help me with my stamps," he muttered to himself. "I'll just have to play sports. It's the only way to get close to him." Daniel dropped the book on the floor and turned on his radio. After a while he fell asleep.

At lunch the next day Daniel knew it was now or never. "Dad?" he said. "I was thinking it might be fun if we shot some baskets. I'm not very good, but . . . "

"Why Daniel," his father answered, his eyes widening. "You want to play basketball? Let me get my sneakers."

As his father left the room, Daniel thought to himself, "Oh no. What have I done?"

His mother winked at him and said, "I'm going shopping. You boys have fun."

The game started off with his father taking five shots and making five baskets. Suddenly he passed the ball to Daniel, who missed it. When Daniel picked it up, he flung it wildly at the basket, but he didn't even hit the backboard.

"You're too far away," his father said. "Dribble in closer, aim, and shoot. It's not hard."

"Right," Daniel said. But under his breath he was saying, "It's not hard for you."

Daniel tried to run and bounce the ball at the same time, but he just couldn't. Finally, in desperation, he threw the ball. This time it hit the roof and rolled down by his father.

"Daniel," his father said frowning, "you're going to have to try harder. Run, jump, and push the ball in. Like this."

Swish. Another basket for Dad.

Daniel was almost ready to cry. He ran, awkwardly bouncing the ball, but just before he shot, he tripped and fell. The ball rolled away.

When Daniel got up, he saw his father looking at his watch. His father said, "What do you say we call it quits? There's a football game on television in a few minutes."

Daniel bent down and pretended to tighten his shoelace. "Okay, Dad," he answered. "Guess I need some more practice."

"You're right," his father answered. "That's all it takes. You ought to come out and shoot baskets with Peter sometime."

"Yea," Daniel mumbled. But he was thinking, "That's one thing I won't do."

The two of them went into the family room, and Daniel's father sat down in his leather chair.

"Turn on Channel 3, will you son?" his father asked.

"Sure," Daniel answered.

After turning on the set, Daniel went back to his father. He leaned against him and the arm of the chair. He wanted to sit next to his father, maybe even on his lap like Peter always did.

Daniel was just starting to relax when his father said, "Hey Daniel, I can't see. Why don't you go over on the couch, and we can both be comfortable."

Daniel moved away and blinked his eyes several times. "Dad," he said, "I don't feel like watching television. I'm going to ride my bike."

"Darn it!" his father answered. "We missed the kickoff—oh—do whatever you want, Daniel."

"I will, Dad," Daniel thought as he walked out of the room. "I will."

Daniel jumped on his bike and rode away. Tears ran down his cheeks, but he didn't care. He thought he might keep on riding forever and never go back. But no. He couldn't leave Mom. She would miss him.

Daniel decided to ride past his teacher's house again. He wouldn't stop or ring the doorbell or anything, but maybe Mr. Johnson would be outside, and Daniel could at least wave to him. It was funny, but on the weekends Daniel kind of missed Mr. Johnson. He was always glad when Monday morning came, and he knew he would see him again.

Daniel turned the corner and grinned a big grin. Mr. Johnson was washing his car in front of the house! He looked up from his work and waved. Daniel waved back and turned into the driveway.

Mr. Johnson looked so different in shorts and a sweatshirt. But his smile was the same, and he looked Daniel right in the eyes like he always did.

"Why Daniel," he said. "What a surprise! Where are you going?"

"Nowhere," Daniel answered. "I'm just out for a ride."

"If you help me finish washing the car, I'll give you some cider. A deal?"

Daniel smiled and said, "It's a deal. I love to help, and I love cider even more."

"Elementary, my dear Daniel," his teacher answered. "You take the hose and squirt the tires, and I'll wipe them with the sponge. We'll be done in no time."

They finished the job in ten minutes, talking and laughing as they worked. It always surprised Daniel how much he had to say to Mr. Johnson.

As they were walking into the house through the garage, Mr. Johnson said, "You know, Daniel, I'm really glad you're in my class. You work hard. You care about other people. And those funny stories you write. They're fantastic."

Daniel didn't know what to say. He was glad Mr. Johnson couldn't see his face. Why would his teacher care about him? His father didn't.

Daniel sat down at the kitchen table, and Mr. Johnson poured them each a big glass of cider. Then Mr. Johnson lifted his glass and said, "Here's to you, Dan. Thanks."

Daniel couldn't stand it anymore. His eyes suddenly became blurry, and he shouted, "Why do you like me so much? My Dad doesn't like me at all. He hates me. I can't help it!"

Daniel pushed the drink away. He put his head down on his folded arms, and he cried and cried. Mr. Johnson didn't say anything, but Daniel heard his chair move closer. Then he felt Mr. Johnson's hand on his back. The hand felt good. It seemed to say it was alright to cry.

After a while Daniel stopped. He raised his head and sat up. Mr. Johnson didn't look surprised. He just handed Daniel a paper towel.

Daniel wiped his face and took a long drink. He felt like telling his teacher everything, and he did. "I'm rotten at sports, and that's all my Dad cares about. My younger brother, Peter, is great at sports, so they're real buddies. They do everything together. I'd rather work on my stamp collection or read or ride my bike. But Dad doesn't care about that stuff. Mom does, but I want Dad too."

"That's rough," said Mr. Johnson, sighing. "I know. But do you ever ask your father to help you do things?"

"Yes, and he's always busy," Daniel answered. "He'd probably help me with my homework. He's kind of proud of my grades. But I can do my work myself."

Mr. Johnson didn't say anything. He seemed to be thinking. Then he smiled and said, "You know, Daniel, I was going to tell everyone tomorrow, but I'll tell you now. You got one of the biggest parts in our play, *Peter Pan*. You're going to be Captain Hook!"

"Oh, wow!" Daniel exclaimed. "I can't believe it? Really? Thanks!"

"You earned the part, Daniel," Mr. Johnson answered. "You were clearly the best for it. You will need a lot of help, though, outside of school, memorizing your lines. Tell your Dad you need his help. Insist if you have to. Many fathers have to be reminded that their children need them. They forget."

"I will. I will!" Daniel answered quickly. He was so excited he could hardly finish his cider. They went outside, and just before Daniel jumped on his bike, he gave Mr. Johnson a pat on the back. Pedaling away, he turned and said, "Thanks a lot. See you Monday."

"You're welcome, Dan, anytime," Mr. Johnson answered.

Daniel couldn't stop smiling as he speeded home. "I'm Captain Hook!" he shouted, startling a robin out of his way. "Mr. Johnson chose me. ME! What if I do stink at sports? Who cares? I'm smart. I'm funny. A lot of people like me. Wait until I tell Dad. Boy will Peter be jealous."

Daniel raced into the family room, and everything was the same. Peter was away. His mother was shopping. His father was still watching television.

"Oh, hi Daniel," his father said. "Where have you been? You missed a great game. I had to watch it by myself."

"I stopped and saw Mr. Johnson," Daniel answered. "We had some cider and talked. I have some great news."

"That was nice of Mr. Johnson," his father said. "But do you think he minded being bothered by a kid on a Saturday afternoon?"

Daniel clenched his fists and said, "You don't understand, Dad. We're friends. I helped him wash his car. Anyway, Dad, Mr. Johnson told me that I'm going to be Captain Hook in our play. It's one of the best parts! Will you help me learn my lines, Dad? I really need you."

"Daniel," his father said, "you're going to be Captain Hook in *Peter Pan?* Can you be that mean? I was never in a play, but I always wanted to be. I guess I could help you with your lines. You'll have a script for me, won't you?"

"I guess so, Dad. I didn't think about that," Daniel answered.

"Well, you have to think about these things," his father said. "Come here. Let me see your arm. Maybe I can make you a hook. Pull your hand inside your sleeve. Good."

Just then they heard a door slam, and Peter burst into the room. When he saw Daniel and their father together, he looked surprised. "What's going on?" he asked.

"Oh, nothing," Daniel answered. "I'm just talking to Dad. I'm going to be Captain Hook in our play at school."

"Big deal," Peter said, shrugging his shoulders. He smiled at their father. "Hey Dad, you want to play football? I'll kick. You receive."

Their father grabbed Peter by the shoulders and said, "Sure Pete. I've been sitting all afternoon. Let's go." He got up from his chair and suddenly looked over at Daniel who was just standing there.

"You want to play, Daniel?" he asked. "It won't be very long."

"No thanks," Daniel answered, sighing and shaking his head. "You guys go play. I'm going to the library and get all the books about *Peter Pan.* That's what I want to do."

"I'll help you later then," his father said, squeezing the back of Daniel's neck lightly. "I'm proud of you."

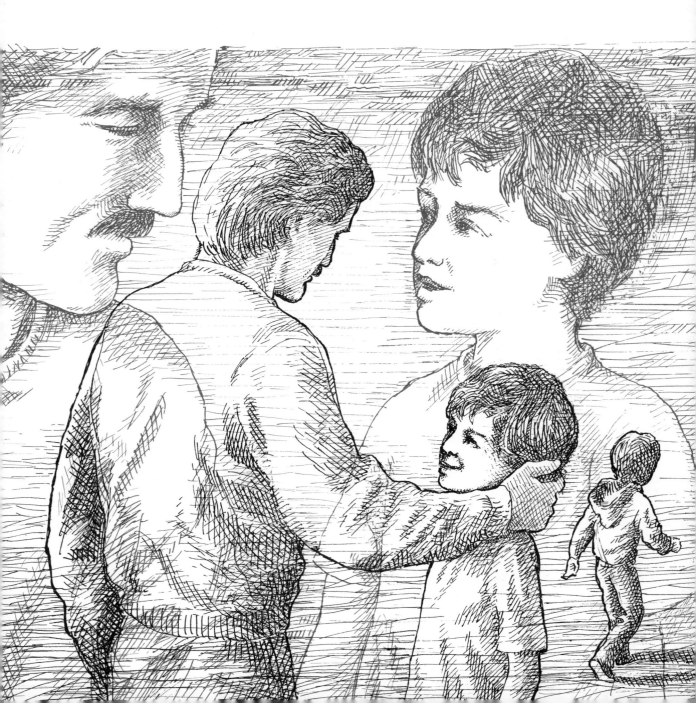

They all went outside, and Daniel hopped on his bike and rode away. As he turned out of the driveway, he looked back and waved. He was smiling again. "I'm going to be the meanest, the slimiest, the scariest captain who ever sailed the seas," Daniel was saying to himself. "And this is just the beginning, just the beginning."